THE FEELING flower

This is Zippy,
Zippy is a feeling flower.

When the morning sun rises,
Zippy feels **CALM** and **RELAXED**.

When the sun is shining brightly,
Zippy feels **HAPPY** and **CHEERFUL**.

Sometimes, too much sun makes Zippy very **HOT**. This makes Zippy feel **ANNOYED** and **UPSET**.

When the wind starts to blow,
Zippy feels **SILLY**.

When the clouds roll in and the sky is overcast,
Zippy starts feeling **TIRED** and **LAZY**.

Sometimes rain makes Zippy feel **UNHAPPY**.

When the sky turns dark and stormy,
Zippy feels very **SCARED**.

But when the rain stops...

and the sky clears,
a rainbow appears...

Zippy feels **BEAUTIFUL** !

What's the weather like outside?

How does it make YOU feel?

THE FEELING flower

about the Author

Leah Dakroub has been writing stories ever since she was 8 years old. She lives with her parents and younger brother in Honolulu, Hawaii. She is homeschooled and enjoys writing, swimming, painting and drawing. At age 10, this is her first published storybook.

Made in the USA
Middletown, DE
19 July 2020